EVEN A BLIND HOG

ROOTS UP AN ACORN

Secrets In The Male Universe

Author: James M. Herald
Illustrated by: James M. Herald

HERALD SOURCE INCORPORATED
PUBLISHING COMPANY
Columbus, Ohio

Library of Congress Cataloging-In-Publication Data

Herald, James Moore

Even A Blind Hog Roots Up An Acorn:
Secrets In The Male Universe

James M. Herald
p. cm

ISBN 0-9648236-9-1
1. Essays. Relationships.
2. Essays: Self-Improvement.
3. Poetry.

Miscellanea.1, Title
CIP: 95-095238

PUBLISHED AND DISTRIBUTED BY:

HERALD SOURCE INCORPORATED
Phone: 614-570-7188
SAN: 298-6868

ISBN 0-9648236-9-1

ACKNOWLEDGMENTS

Thank you all and each.

ABOUT THE AUTHOR

JMHerald at 49, drinks a few sacred beers, smokes a few Holy cigarettes and goes to Blessed Bars.

EVEN A BLIND HOG...

SECRETS IN THE MALE UNIVERSE

TABLE OF CONTENTS

THE START

This is how it all started
101 FM
thanks for playing Come Dancing at 9:30 pm Tuesday
3/30/93
The Kinks had great tunes

When you enter this world there is only
one thing to be

Patient

If You make it to the W's
you may make it to the Y's
and with a little luck to the Z's
and end up
any one of the various
Tropical Americas Weevils of
the genus Zzzzvra often
destructive to plants

but that won't stop you from
eating them will it

One must graze, eh.
you vegetarian you
You treacherous vicious killer
vegetarians
You can't hear their crys
                    Moooo

So I'm
sitting around
thinking about
going to

a bar after 7 beers and fourscore and six years
Spring Fed Couples
walking past
wondering when
two is worse than none
one on one

Hell fuck Judge its only Tuesday
get their too early in the week and
you start to judge yourself

who needs the others

You can't even hear them

Silent Scream is not a sound
it is a not
It is a way away a way
dont insult the thing far
by attaching it to a-way

My brother the surgeon knows the word
insult
I insulted into this patient aren't we

patient

aren't we

The wait always the weight
but make no mistake about it
He is a healer
The weight is the wait

(there was a time
I take pen in hand
I trust this finds you well

get off the girls you
cocksucking motherfuckers
just get off the girls or
I will be the next person you see
standing at your door
at a most inconvenient time
possibly upset.)

But, actually, they dont need me
They have already addressed me you

Patience

Even a blind hog
roots up an acorn

So I am
sitting around
having a few beers
(But I will be
standing at your door
dont mis-remember)

Just Columbus Ohio
3/30/93
Cold and Clear
french fry old wood fire
new Spring soil margarine factory night

it is always the smells

I miss the Steel mills
like you people miss a UFO

SURVEY SAYS

10% of all us users of the following substances are abusers and addicted:

booze
drugs
cigarettes
sex
anger
hate
love
belief
dis-belief
non-belief
vegetables
outdoors
indoors
fitness
fatness
work
play
manipulation
deceit
truth
honesty
integrity
wife
husband
father
mother
children
travel
home
togetherness
aloneness

light
dark
humor
toys
cars
shopping
shoes
shirts
skirts
birds
dogs
cats
politics
team
family
civilian
military
celebrity
obscurity
state
nation
Irish
Italian
Serb
Croat
house
land
water
fire
oil
life
death.

BOY

Never sleep alone

In every category
120 males to every
100 females

go to the dreams
boy

go to the dreams

both of them.

EIGHT OR NINE

I'll tell you what
all men miss
they see it from their cars

he's carrying a helmet
with pants a little large
wandering back from the game
he's used up all backyards

he's in between
>   the coaches
>   the school
>   the house
>   the guards

at last some time
to just himself
released
from all the bars.

PETS

You better keep feeding it
All unconditional love has its price.

MEN

Darling Honey Dear

no Dog is one dimensional
you buy them
acquire them

ask them to
protect you
affection you

Leash them
walk them
they stop

Sometimes to smell to wet to bark to pull

Surprised

You who claim intuition

the stop was it
inthewrong
inappropriate
embarrassing

Let them at it
the trees
the walk
the ground
the run
the smell
the wet
the bark
the pull

Its just a dog.

MANHOOD

What a wimp
She said
He wouldn't say it to him so
I did
I went right up to him and
I said it

Yeah
(I thought)
One small point
you did not have to weigh that one
pre eminent consequence attached
to such a say
Having an immediate intimate relationship
suddenly develop
between
your face and
that floor.

GENTLEMEN

Male Gorillas are
Gentlemen
we are not

They are
    strong
    fierce
    full of power
We are
    strong
    fierce
    full of power

They are
Gentlemen
we are not

They protect provide sustain
we protect provide sustain

But they are
Gentle
men

and we are not.

FATHERHOOD

What do you say to this small thing
That now you call your son

Befuddled are you Dad
as you watch him romp and run

he looks or acts just like you
or perhaps his mom

But deep within your fearful soul
you're sure he's neither one

In one respect he's just like you
a master mimic growing

will you enforce a duplicate
or allow for his own knowing.

SONS (STEAL)

out of the Earth it came
mined and smelted
by your gentle father
who loved you

worked for 30 years
in the heat and graphite rain
summer and winter
he made that steel

so you could live

sure enough that steel
went to be fabricated
and wrapped itself
around that shell

that shell

off it went
to the front lines
into that big gun
a projectile now

rammed into that barrel
by the sons of another
trained in the art
the art of projectile
projection

and sure enough
out of that Barrel it flew
on the wings of
black powder

black powder out of the
Earth

and the Earth
it struck and that steel
made by your gentle father

exploded into a
million pieces
one of which found the body of a
cherished son

killed him

into the Earth he went
with a hole in his heart
buried to be the
Earth

Sure enough he waits

for some one's
gentle father
who loves
to bring it
to steal again

from him to you
with love.

COACHES

A quitter never wins
A winner never quits

I quit wearing underwear
I quit wearing ties
I quit wearing watches
I quit shaving
I quit swearing
I quit lying
I quit blaming
I quit hating
I quit fearing

I quit winning
I quit wins

I quit

FAGS

Standing at the Bar
three hours or more
Waiting for another round.
in the thousand yard stare

He said

There was a time
when what we call fags
were asexual beings
they were the chosen people of God
In ancient times
such beings were forced to choose sexuality
that is the choice they made

Without missing a beat.

TROOPS

Clicked off the T.V.
sat in the dark

heard it again
took a walk in the Park

applied to an army squad
Before this to a business
Before this to a neighborhood
before this to a town
before this to a church
before this to a boxing camp
before this to a police precinct
before this to a movie set
and before this to a situation comedy cast

We are like family they say

Like family

Whos mom whos dad
whos brother whos sister
whos happy whos sad
whos cousin whos uncle
whos outlaw whos aunt
whos favorite whos special
who can do who cant

whos grandma whos grandpa
whos daughter whos son
who keeps it all working
who has all the fun

whos wife whos husband
whos girlfriend whos tramp
who does the clean up
whos the cement

whos the provider
whos at the helm
who wields the power
who holds the home

who sits there waiting
watching to see
wholl be the first
to suddenly flee.

Company unmarkets
customers nil
towns en bankrupt
champs over the hill
teams all ashambles
nary a win
churches in scandal
invaded by sin

police force enforcing
ethnics are near
neighborhoods dangerous
we're outta here

sitcoms been cancelled
movies a bust
Platoons done a killing
equipments arust

who is like family
at home or outside
where is the family
claimed with such pride

family ah family
what does it mean
it's really a nothing
merely a dream

We search and we find
families no end
or maybe produce one
and fertility spend

Then it is mine
us you and me
against all the others

Like Family

THE LETTER (4/10/93)

He was 18. First year in college. Studying ceramics
He wrote a letter. He said:

My mom and dad are pretty cool
I respect them immensely but
I seem to have more & more
trouble relating to them

I guess they are just a lot too
uptight for me they can't relax
just kick back and say
what the Fuck

This major difference in our personalities
causes some tension when I'm home
for extended periods of time
at the moment
I'm kind of lost

I don't really want the year to end but
I don't want it to keep going
I don't really feel like going home but
there is nowhere else to go so

I'm stuck at home for 3 months
        AHHH

So anyway if you have any incredibly great advice or actually
anything you feel like sharing with me
Go ahead and fill me in

I used to think I had some clue but
the more I learn
the less I know
I think.

THE REPLY (4-10-93)

At 46 and 3/4, the reply:

Thanks for THE LETTER
What a pleasant surprise
I want to address some of the things
your letter brought to me

Please understand
I have no investment in this say
nor does it require your
reading it
agreeing to it
responding to it or to me

Although
there is no wrong and
there is no right
I am able to say this
Everything that follows may be
wrong
it is meant only for your
consideration

Perhaps
in the fabric of it
you will find
what people call answers
Perhaps

HOME

There is no home except in the self
Listen to your self.

That requires paying attention to
what you pay attention to

Pre serve your self first
and necessarily you will provide
the fertile ground
for all other selfs

Therefore be self ish
You will then speak with accuracy
Definitional truth
will not be an issue

GIFTS

The giving of a gift is for the self of the giver
Once a gift is offered
the Receiver may do with it
what they please

Any judgment
by the giver with regard to the Receiver's
acceptance or use of the offered gift does
damage to the self of the giver

PROMISES

There is no such thing as a promise.

Assessing yourself or others
on the basis of promises
does damage to intrinsic forgiveness
and to your self

25

LOVE

LOVE
is a definitional term
perhaps if we substitute the word
WANT
whenever we use the term
LOVE
we will understand why we employ the term
LOVE
LOVE
just is
Love
Love
requires no use

FORGIVENESS

No ONE
possesses the power to
FORGIVE
it is not a power held one over another
Forgiveness
just is
LISTEN
to your self
you will hear
it
sound
is
LOVE
and
They are not separate
They are not in GOD
They are not outside of your self
They are organic

Like the materials that contribute
to the product you call ceramics.

SEX

SEX is
intrinsically innocent
and
a biological function that carries as part of it
pleasure

Pay attention
when you have the opportunity to engage in it
it is the one experience that gives access to the
4th Dimension

Watch
it is a glimpse into the dimension we have
attributed to God

Swim
in that sea free fall into that atmosphere

Dance
with it and honor all those who participate with you
you will then know
Innocence.

SEX AND DISEASE

DIS ease
associated with sex
does not come from
sex
that which feeds upon
hate
anger
jealousy
fear
has attached disease to

Sex
the thing that feeds
cannot touch the
intrinsic beauty and power of
sex
or remove it from our world
the human species host would cease
it can only infect it
with
fear jealousy anger hate
dis ease
its food supply
when we are blessed to acknowledge
the inherent innocence of
sex
that food supply will cease
we will survive
that which feeds will
die.

FEAR

All ways embrace
fear
Recognize it as the source of
anger
hate
possession
envy
jealousy
and dance with it
all ways dance with
fear
Patience
in all ways you are protected
action

if any will be revealed
Listen

Man is God afraid.

HURT

No one
carries the Power to
hurt
you
you
gift that Power to an other out of
fear

LONELINESS

Trust
that you are always
alone
alone ness is not loneliness
alone ness is the gift given
to allow us to listen to
our selfs
each of us
will never cease to pre serve our aloneness
our selfs
no matter if the talk is of my
family
children
husband
wife
team
company
religion
city
state
country

allow for it.

RECEIVER

Look at this gift of
aloneness
as it operates in
yourself in others and
honor
it
illuminates
gift
you will know
when you gift
your self you
alone
are permitted to assess that
gift
it may not look like a
gift
to the
receiver

PARENTS

Your Parents are individual
selfs
called
MOM
DAD
Roles
There is no training for these
Roles
It is on the job
They have only their
own experience and the
bombardment of culture
This is not training the
self

trains
They strain to hear them
selfs
50 years and 57 years is a function only of
chronology
Like you Like me they strain to hear them
selfs
allow for this in
them
and you necessarily allow for it in
you
your self

FRIENDS

There is
no
such thing as
friend
enemy
all persons are your
teachers
Listen
to what each calls up in you

ALL OF US

Patience
Parents you and me all of us are
together
in the dance with
fear
Listen
to them strain to hear them
selfs
you will necessarily understand each's
value

is the highest
value

COURAGE

You are allowed to
Stand
wherever and whenever you
choose
Other selfs assessments have no power unless you
gift
it to
them.

I have the power to
say
I
say
NO MORE MR. NICE GUY DO YOU
SEE

SPRING

Spring
is her
go out mboy and enjoy
Spring
Alcohol
tobacco
marijuana
peyote
mushrooms
LSD
are substances that alter consciousness
allow for glimpses into other realms
do not judge

Each
is organic like ceramics
Pre serve above all else your own power your
self
only you can
gift
that power to some thing out side of your
self
including drugs

OLD FRIENDS

Fear
I
are
old friends
I
gift it a name
so when it talks in my
head
I
fear
cannot hide there

it is not female

THIS IS MY
SAY.

NIECES

LISA

I come when she calls
I do what she says
No matter how tired
No matter what's said

I met her in diapers
on her not on me
she had turned one
me forty three

I was close she was crying
rendered my heart
all terror confusion
Just tore me apart

Abandoned the cry said
lost without home
No one to help me
I'm left all alone

Twas only a bedroom
at Grandma's its true
to her it was dungeons
blackness and cruel

Were it a castle
with hundreds of men
I'd charge and I'd cut
take many a head
to save the fair Lisa
from fear and from dread

Yet took only a light switch
no charger I'd need
her widened eyes questioned
am I now freed

I reached down I held her
streaked tears on her face
And whispered its O.K.
It's me dear you're safe

There were no dungeons
no dragon no harm
your parents are close by
no cause for alarm

This child is not mine
as we say around here
my title is Uncle
let's keep that quite clear

But if dragons do come
hissing fear breathing hate
and move near this damsel
claiming license by fate

Upon that Black Charger
Full armed I will ride
and cut slash and bleed them
til death death they cry.

PERFECTION
(Mother & Child Reunion)

Got your letter

Call her by her original name
not my
or mother
or my mother

Seductress you called alcohol
Curiously you made it feminine
or maybe not so curious

Interesting isn't it
how anything one finds attractive
when defined as bad
gets to be a seducer and
therefore feminine

Seduction
implies some kind of sexual interaction
doesn't it

often alcohol and sexual interaction
are used in concert with one another

Please indicate in the box provided
which of the following list occurs with
participation in each or both.

❑ Release
❑ surrender
❑ vulnerability
❑ power
❑ euphoria
❑ electricity

- ❏ pleasure
- ❏ healing
- ❏ security
- ❏ forgetting
- ❏ remembering
- ❏ insight
- ❏ sleep
- ❏ rest
- ❏ peace

Pluses

I leave it to you to list the downside
the damaging parts of each or both

Why would any one choose the use the abuse
of alcohol and or sexual interaction
Each can kill the body

Your inquiry has attached alcohol to
mother
my mother

Why would any one choose the use the abuse
of alcohol

perhaps because there is
an allowance for the use of alcohol

If alcohol is ones only
unrestricted access to the
Pluses
Perhaps any one will accept
the downside of
use and abuse

Each Entity in this world
holds the power to get
alcohol

How many opportunities to access the
PLUSES
are available in our world our dimension outside of
sexual interaction & alcohol

all other non seductive alternatives
mirror each but without such apparent
ease and palatable pleasure.

Try this list:

- ❑ meditation
- ❑ religion
- ❑ spirituality
- ❑ belief
- ❑ Financial power
- ❑ political power
- ❑ humility
- ❑ forgiveness
- ❑ understanding
- ❑ love giving understanding
- ❑ being the answer for others
- ❑ Living on a mountain

And ask where each any all or any combination
will access all of the
Pluses

However this is not about
you or
sex or
alcohol or
a designed denunciation or condonation of
any each or all

38

It is about Intrinsic Understanding

my
mother
my mother

has not been seduced by alcohol
It is an Entity choice
Is her choice any better than
yours or mine

She has gifts
where have they been allowed unrestricted right
to be and develop
where have been the choices to access the
PLUSES

Perhaps
Spirituality
Sexual Interaction
Alcohol

When she stood outside of
the Earth developed systems
and saw her choices
She tried all three

Which do you think gave her access to the
PLUSES
unrestricted
uncensored
available
to her own choice
with no gender application

The downside of alcohol could not hold a candle to the up

Perhaps selfish but
what is most valuable to the self
Feeding nurturing the self
adds value to all selfs

feeding nurturing the self
does not equal body survival
Self ish ness
is
not death to Society

She is allowed to be self ish
we all demand it for our selfs

Her choice alcohol
had the downside

You the child the daughter child
lived in both the up and
downside of her choice

But you remember
and you fear
the downside of her choice

Because her choice
allowed for the non priority of
your self
an attack upon
your self

Perhaps that attack upon
your self
is a mutation of
Intrinsic Love

If you are a Saudi Woman
my
mother
my mother

with a female child
would you not
acquiesce
allow for
appear to support
the killing of the female child

out of Love

knowing that what awaited the daughter
the child her self
is that culture
(which does not even include the monster
alcohol)

In our culture to a much more
murky
confused
degree is not
Mother
charged with that Responsibility

Kill that which will harm the child
the daughter self

And when Mothers aim is
murky
confused
BAD
what does mother hit

The Saudi Mother
has it easy
Her act of allowance
does not require aim nor
the Responsibility of aim

How would you aim that weapon
in your mothers place with
her aim
after having
her mothers aim
and her
her mothers aim
and her
her mothers aim
and her
her mothers aim

How is your aim

Alcohol is access
MOTHER is Intrinsic Love
Neither is gender specific

you
the female
hold mother
you
the female
claim mother

Exclusively

You that claim MOTHER
Live in FEAR of
BAD AIM

Why do you claim Mother
Producer does not equal Mother

As your producer
is now charged with
my
mother
my mother

Re-member

it takes some degree of courage
to take on Mother with
Bad light
Bad eyes
Bad aim

And the Culture yelling
shoot shoot shoot
kill that which will
harm the daughter self

The Intuitive self is the place
where there are no
beliefs or distractions
mutations or classifications
restrictions or limitations

The Intuitive self is the place
where there are no
definitional morals
definitional mores
definitional ethics
definitional understanding
definitional love

The Intuitive self is the place
where there is no Cultural Yelling

It is where the
PLUSES LIVE

And Sexual Interaction
and alcohol
and mind altering substances
each or all can and do
offer access to all the
PLUSES

Imperfect
BAD
Perhaps

But a Gentle man
that I heard of
held in the highest esteem
in certain circles

With his next to
next to
next to
last breath

when asked what he wanted
to quench his thirst
It is said that he answered

Wine with a splash...up.

TRANSPORTATION SECTION

TURN SIGNALS

A promise
is the blinking turn signal flashing
from the on coming car of life

DEFENSIVE DRIVING

Interstate 71 going south
overtaking clumps of cars
huddled against
the threat
the dreaded predator
the Ohio State Highway Patrol

Risking all jeopardy of
mile per hour closeness
Ever alert
Ever asleep

While Ohio in its
Early autumn glory
rushes alongside
motionless

There's one they caught one
Like Wildebeest they watch the feast

Relief

Return to the herd

TRAFFIC LIGHTS

Where I live they are the sea
I mean they sound in the sea

Green - like surf they come
Yellow - and pass and pause
Red - soundless breathless

Green
Yellow
Red

Green
Yellow
Red

Green yellow red
Day through night
Night through day

My rhythm
My sea

My woody's outside covered with snow

SWITCHES

In this world
you can operate at 1/2 power
and be a success

at 1/4 power
you can rule the world

on off
they'll make you a god.

GREYHOUNDS

Back in the Autumn of 92
I jumped on the dog
to get to you

Wasn't cute and
it wasn't chic
My car was out cold
I was in heat

At Y-Town's station
by seven a.m.
dropped there by car
and a long found friend

(Afraid of the bus?
was the out send)

This is for LowLifes
the small the nots
They ride in their cars
shoot block to block

They take the Dog
cause it runs to where
they want to go and
gets them there

What in the hell
am I doing here

(Well you're on the Dog
I suppose to insure
that you arrive
and get at the cure)

Sat myself down
clutched at my bag
looked all around
and tried to sag

Off we roared
down streets never seen
(You see I first left
old Y-Town
when I was eighteen)

Going two hundred miles
off to the South
with memories of sticking
my dick in that mouth

Decided to look-mmmm
all around
at the folks who as me
were all outward bound

Beings Human they were
some black and some grey
Scattered about in that
coach on this day

They watched with me
Ohio rumbling by
ablaze in the autumn
accented by sky

We stopped in Heath
Akron and Dover
Mansfield's to come
East Liverpools over

Out came the lunches
the food and the snacks
All of the necessaries
I'd forgotten to pack

(What would I do
What did I know
I was all get there
they were the show)

Strange as it seems
hard to imagine
but ribs I was offered
with reckless abandon

Got to laugh and to watch
listen and eat
with no need to leave
the safety (my seat)

The Driver he drove
and was the machine
guess he was used to
this remarkable scene

Don't need to tell you
physics it wins
Speed time and distance
and Columbus we're in

(Forgot what I'm after
Didn't seem true
all of this want
directed at you)

Pulled myself off
Caught me my grip

Decided to walk home
Just part of the trip

Took all of an hour
I didn't care
Stepped on the porch
no one was there

Looked at the phone
Why pick it up
Found an old butt
and lit it up

Travel yes Travel
by boat car and plane
but takin the Dog
is the name of the game

HEY GIRLS

Actually, if you really
want to meet men
stop by a Jiffy Lube
between 10:30 a.m. and 3:30 p.m.
anytime after Oct. 15 and before Nov. 30

It helps if they're having a special

Pull up a chair.

Don't forget your car.

MASS TRANSIT

They file in
usually around 10 p.m.

By 11:30 the place is jammed
all that brightness
that energy
that talent
color and beauty

Suburbs bound

Loops and lawns
cul de sacs and two car garages
wait
They are jobbed
and or colleged
colleged and or jobbed

Looking for that
right one
to come along
and ride that train
suburbs bound

Where else can they go

FLYING
(OUT VS. IN)

The Stars are always out

Though best seen at night
I'm told

Flying West to the Left Coast
Looking down
Way past Kansas
Probably Nevada

Islands of Light
Ocean of Dark

The stars are out

Hey
down there
HEY

But you are in

ACROSS THE UNIVERSE

I stood
one early chill Spring morning
in the sun
hands in my pockets
as the warm so long gone
Returned

And stared into the sidewalk
emptyfull
watching feeling the warm
on my back

Forty years later
on this day

I stood
one early chill autumn morning
in the sun
hands in my pockets
as the warm so long here
Departed

And stared into the sidewalk
emptyfull
watching feeling the warm
on my back

Crossing timespace I
armheld
that boy so long gone

We stood
watchfelt the warm on our backs
and stared into the sidewalk

Together

INTO SHAPE

Working out

the other day
started to weep
right in the middle of my third set of curls

Just started to cry

No reason just sobbed
while finishing my third set of curls

Working out

BREATHING

Looked up
Cynic
in Websters Dictionary Copyright 1916-1959 pg 206

One of the Greek school of
Philosophers who taught that
Virtue
is the only good and that its
Essence
lies in self-control and
Independence
Later cynics were violent critics of
current customs and current philosophers
Hence a faultfinding captious critic a
misanthrope

It's even more amusing to look up
Apology
Use an old dictionary

IN THE BEGINNING WAS THE WORD
and Buddy
THE WORD IS GOD

WARNING
Look them up before each use
Consider the motive for each use
Each is like oil based paint
While considering you may get a chance to take
a breath

CAREFUL
this hazardous pause may allow for
listening

WALKING

June
night
windy
leaves
singing
I love you (it them him her that)
Love iz is
I hate you (it them him her that)
Hate iz is
I fear you (it them him her that)
Fear iz is

Is is iz is iz
isn't it

AIRCONDITIONING

Thirty years from now
we will be told that
all that damn air conditioning
was well ah
Bad for you

Ensealed into those storied buildings
with nary a window to lift
was well ah
Bad for you

Enclosed in those frigerated cars
vacuumed packed for freshness
was well ah
Bad for you

Inslated in those clammy homes
distressed at that rogue fly
(how'd he get in here)
Was well ah
Bad for you

What we needed (we will be told) were
doors to open
porches to sit on
windows to raise
swings to swing
sidewalks to walk
get outside in
get inside out

See (we will be told) you were supposed to
sweat
slow down
take it easy
take a nap

hear a cricket
hear a voice
see a star
swat that fly

Air conditioning (we will be told) was actually
a plot
a plan
a design
to keep you from knowing an other
inside out
outside in

Air conditioning (we will be told)
also had all of those serious
health consequences you all are now suffering

Sorry

We just found out (we will be told)

But we certainly are pleased that
you all quit eating those fatty foods

which by the way turns out (we will be told)
were ah well actually kind of sort of

good for you

THE GREAT OUTDOORS

Sometimes I sleep on the Porch

Not the way you might think

Isn't always summer
sometimes fall
even winter

In winter though I have a coat

Head drops
cigarette dangles
beers at half mast

But I'm still sleeping outside
(on the Porch)

Ain't dead yet

WILDERNESS (QUOTE)

When I told my Mam & Pap
I was going to the mountains
to be a mountain man

They acted like they was gut shot

They said
That's where all the wild critters
and savages live

            Del Que
               in movie <u>Jeremiah Johnson</u>
            John Millius
               Writer/Author

BANDIT

He watched me
not even moving his head
Rolled back comes to mind

Anita wrote from England
Its an old Arab trick
blow across his nostrils

Met her twenty years ago
Semi-Amish Ohio farm raised
I knew she knew so I blew
He tossed his head

But he danced and he pranced
and he jumped and he seethed
and he heaved and tried
and he ran like the wind

I take Bandit when I
want to impress the girls
he said
Bandit has his own
I thought

New bit gives more control
he said
Bandit has his own
I thought

You who want to lie in women
or perhaps re lie in men
Might mount the young Bandit
to know what's ahead

I dream often of Bandit

see him where he is not
and think of all that trembles
where lives the lives that's caught

To release from out the stable
six by six by nine
and run and prance and scramble
then return again to dine

So I swing onto the saddle
feeling blessed before my time
and told the gods to ride with me
and survive this unnamed crime

to ask a thing to carry me
to run and prance and climb
the hill to almost nowhere
when I's way past my prime

But carry was his burden
his choice
his life
his time

all he wanted was
the chance to
run and prance and climb

So who's to say what's courage
what's fear and what is kind
I say get on ole Bandit
If answers you will find

With luck you'll get some feeling
some sense some touch some sight
and know at last what is free
what's caught and what is light

Take a chance to prance and dance
and run up on a hill
to scramble always scramble
and then at last be still

THE HUNT

If I could leave a
scent trail

like cats or
deer or
any critter

so they could
find me

after they drink and
talk that
serious
understanding
empathetic
supportive
compassionate
talk
and after they eat
and after they are full
when they look around Empty

sniff
and find the scent trail

and me.

DESTINATIONS

Watching the old friends
First Avenue they meet

Exchanging warm how are yous
Shake hands then shuffle feet

Enjoying each the other
while standing in the street

The hardened Mask is melted
the meeting such a treat

For over one half hour
together they exchange
past histories and presents
exhibit quite a range

But comes the time
when going on
gnaws at each's head

goodbye is now appropriate
reluctantly they spread
and turn away forgetting
destinations just ahead

that hardened mask like Magic
makes a quick return

reclaims its territory
took so long to learn

Lesson upon Lesson
we all attend that school

walk around a smiling
it only makes a fool

69

IGNORANCE IS NO EXCUSE

Law
Intrinsic
Lives

on the swords edge
on the razors edge

Between
fear and
Desire

THE JUDGE

Some who claim the right to say
will say that was a long time ago

Some voice that speaks in Jennifer's head
says she has
fear and doubt
loneliness and pain
uncertainty and darkness

To this voice that makes this say
I laugh and rub my hands
for these prevarications
dictate you take the stand

get up there you motherfucker
sit - YOUR DARKNESS - down
it's time to take a real clear look
before your seeds are sewn

The evidence is all that talks
not your bullshit voice
I offer it to this court
and it can made the choice

Jennifer is not a role
though roles she has performed
daughter sister wife and mother
She surely comes adorned

Exhibits one through four
I label each of them
and put them here before this court
to still that voice within

Preponderance of evidence
is required here
because those lying words you speak
spew poison in her ear

Now consider Jennifer
all of five years old
alone she was and the first
when fear it lost the hold

Took on school and all unknowns
white shoes upon her feet
and never stopped arunning
her middle name compete

She never stopped
and will not stop
until she is complete

She was alone
as is all firsts
though allies she did find

and loneliness is just a word
authored by your kind

of doubt and uncertainty
are what you have to say
but She relied upon Her heart
Her love
Her self
Her way

You look at what came through Her around
about and by
a garden world of Life and Strength
the facts they do not lie

73

Now will this court require me
to identify them all
each seed each plant each flower
that grows within Her walls

(the pictures files and papers are
stacked out in the hall)

I ask this Court to ORDER
this lying voice to cease
and end it for all time
I call for its decease.

"Your exhibits are well taken
the evidence is clear
it is not required
that you continue here

The Voice must end its speeches its
darkness and its pain
and to ensure it does
this sentence is ordained:

You VOICE

will no longer speak to Her
Jennifer by name
I condemn you to the Void
where no sound sustains

Further it is ORDERED
if attempted to return
Future parole is revoked
assuredly you'll burn

You're free to go My Jennifer
to enjoy each day
I heard it was your Birthday
Go forth without delay

Before you are the open fields
the sun the wind the light
your innocence has claimed them you
fought the valiant fight

Re-member My Jennifer
white shoes upon your feet
and how you
laughed
ran and
played

(although I said compete)

These fields that are before you
are yours and yours alone
you have the right so play there
because they are your Home."

It is so ORDERED ADJUDGED AND
DECREED
Effective Date: January 20, 1995.

The Judge

EVIDENCE

Please count them all
they stand on the Porch
where I do not stand

                Bottles Beer
                Bottles Beer

Count them so you will know
I drank them

                one and all
                one and all

and saw into the sea
into the see

I thank them

                one and all
                one and all

and the gods that let them be

MONEY

The hard part is getting born
with 3 years to play before
school
learning
job
mate
30 years avoiding
ice cream
red meat
other unqualified humans

Turning 60

Opening the door one frosty morning
stepping outside
without a coat

ENEMIES

Out of the Cold
and the Dark
They come

Bent forward
Against the wind
The snow

Solitary
graying
shape changing

From
The North
The South
The West
The East

Relentlessly trudging
to the Oasis
of light

You watch.
There is no

WHERE

to go

until the Big Bear check out girl
finishes bagging your groceries

CRYING

You know
Don't you
Each time

You weep in
Your body rocks
And tears brim
Your eyes
You bring into being

glistening
healing
magic

Like a faerie to dance
in the evening air
Like swirling snowflakes
in a street light

You have seen them
haven't you now
without

paints
  or
prose
  or
poetry
  or
instruments
  or
gifts
  or
training
  or
credentials
  or
trying

Talent

TALENT

You know don't you

Each time you laugh in and
your body rocks and
tears brim your eyes

You bring into being
glistening healing magic

Like a faerie

To dance in the evening air
Fireflies
Perhaps swirling
snow flakes
in a streetlight

You have seen them haven't you now without
paints or prose
poetry or instruments
gifts or training
credentials or trying

Talent

VOICES

So I said to the voice
Give me some peace
For now I am leaving
There will be no trace

For wanting to kill
is right for this place

And I am for killing
and not after grace

Don't want to add to
This human race

Oh? And what about pizza
burgers and shakes

And what about Halloween
The leaves moon Frosts Lace

And what about summer
The knights warm the lakes

You know that a killing
is really no choice
it just frees that spirit
This said the voice

But if its an evil
a hate sought to end
Kill that which lives in
holds hostage his head

For innocent he is
and she them and it

Strike true with your sword
and you surely will hit

Fear lurking inside there
which calls to your aim
The sword is forgiveness
The lurker is slain

SONGS

When I have the money
and step outside the race
I get me 24 long neck Buds
just   I guess   in case

FIll up old Amana
never so secure
as when there's 12 more left
in cooling sinecure

The'windows doors wide open
the smells the breeze the sounds
crickets dogs and buses
the senses all astound

Radio on I know these songs
so far away in years
but close enough to qualify
for horshoes grenades my ears:

Are the stars out tonight
I don't care if its cloudy or bright

I only have eyes for you dear

you are hear
so am I

maybe millions of people go bye
But they all disappear from vu

And eye only have
I's
for you.

MUSIC

My sister Jeannie
she said

perhaps tie the
words to music
as she has seen my
guitar.

She sees so much
for me
so much

I love each of them
Jeannie
the words
music

ain't no music
ain't no words
ain't no brother

Just a man

the walk alone will kill you

PIANO LESSONS

Men must be
simultaneously
the threat to women and the protector of women

Women must be
simultaneously
the holders of sexuality and the disparagers of sexuality

Each in himself
Each in herself
or in others
depending upon who or what each wants to play
and the why for the playing

Watching the performance the self marvels at the
dexterity
nimbleness
dedication
inventiveness
structure
of this discipline

and acknowledges the Centuries of
practice
practice
practice

But there is no music.

MAGIC

Jeez
Every day
watching the TV
Turning on the lights
Driving the car
Watching the airplane
Suffering the helicopter
Answering the phone
on and on and on

Whatever happened to magic

Ahna nathrak oofus bethood dothyell dyendvey

The Charm of Making

SORCERERS

Merlin where the hell are you

he said: it was a sign
       she told me it was a sign

he said: your sign or her sign

he said: our sign

he said: is she your Merlin
       does your Merlin see the sign
       read the sign

Merlin my Merlin

where the hell are you

WEREWOLVES OF LONDON

I saw them tonight

The Dark Ones

Sitting along the wall
where no one else would sit
brooding
watching
menacing
creeping
to the food that nourishes them

I have heard them called
Demons
Vampires
Devils
but there is no title just

The Dark Ones

All prey there felt them
All prey there saw them
All prey there knew them
No prey there would look at move against

The Dark Ones

Then
Suddenly
Two Ohio Girls came in
Glowing
Radiant
Rooted
in the purity of past fucks and
stopped them cold

89

2 small light beings innocent
fearlessly took their food

No man there saw them recede
No man there saw them retreat
No man there saw them withdraw

The Dark Ones were just gone

Starving they walk the night
and I walk the night

So long as I live
so long as I breathe
so long as I walk

The Dark Ones will not own the night.

ALIENS

Tonight he cannot join them
in bars he loves so well
his presence is like atrophine
it holds them in a spell

They see him there in pleasure
a comrade he must be
but a bit disturbing
when sits right next to me

So now I wait Septembered
and watch the full moon rise
and drink a long neck bottle
it's bud to be so wise

I'll smoke my cigaretto
an Indian it's called
and wish I could be in that bar
with patrons one & all

(across that bar upon that stool right against that wall)

in my cups is sacred
as sacred as the Grail
you chase at what your after

my Foot has found its rail.

NICKNAMES (Chris/topher)

Now it's dark
the last good day
before the Hawk arrives

I sit myself
out on the porch
ass stride said moon arise

crack that beer
light that butt
foot upon that rail

and listen nightfull voices
that call to no avail

watching passing cars
wayed to no place near
all thoughts upon The Toph
his word
his voice
his cheer

and wish I could be with him
just to say his hear:

Coony you old sonofabitch
How'd you get out here.

U.F.O.'S

Waiting for the invasion
The
Allpowerful
allknowing
otherworld
to impose upon us
peace
understanding
togetherness

Teach us how to use
Show us how to distribute
all of the Blessings
of this Earth
Upon all beings

Better talk to the Indians first

CONTROL

It

Starts with a breeeeze
(and in summer when you need it most)

you glance up

The windchimes sing a dischordant song,
The screen door creaks and slams
the leaves go silver the papers fly

Damn

The Wind

MANNERS

The Introduction
to fear
comes early
swaddling clothes
early

There you lay
giants
lean into your world
leering their
right
to lean into your world

Mommy
Daddy
Grandpa
Grandma
Uncle
Aunt
Neighbor
Friend

who the hell do they think they are

You are the one who came in courage

helplessly
fearlessly
in courage

CHOICES

Watched it fall all day
and all night
In the Park the light
from the old fashioned street lamp
cast a perfect glistening circle
undisturbed by foot or paw

It Blew off the roofs
and the tops of the knolls
drifting deep in the swales
muffling all sound

Easier to walk the knolls
but wind reaches you there
Harder to slog the swales
but no wind no wind

choices

REST

Asked the Drink
about my
dead sister

we were Irish twins
I said

It's an old joke
the Irish twins
part

The rest of it
The rest of it

ain't no joke.

QUIET

It sounds now in
sirens
voices
traffic

There was a time when night was in the country
not like you imagine in the country just not
sirens
voices
traffic

But not silence

Hold your breath
stick your head under water
and listen

That is silence

HUMANITARIANISM

I caught a warm

probably from touching that girl who smiled
maybe stayed out too long on that sunny day
could be the night when I laughed too much

Who knows

So I tried to exercise up

First walking
Then running
Then swimming

But the warm it hung on

Familiar with the old adage
Drink a cold
Smoke a fever

I figured the combination would handle this warm

About eight off to the local Tavern I did repair
to insure I covered every remedy

They say neglecting a warm can be dangerous
which leads to other more serious complications

arriving I discovered how bad this warm was
there were a lot of people there

It was really going around

These people they were smoking and drinking allright
but had added variations and permutations

talking and laughing
musicing and dancing

noticed the dancing most
guess it was because mostly the girls were doing it

Anyway I
stayed and watched
talked and laughed
musiced and danced

All the things I was supposed to do plus some

And the warm went away for awhile
but it keeps coming back apparently a

Chronic condition

So I am still hard at it finding the cure
Scientifically you can be sure
wouldn't want this warm to go unchecked
and infect the general population

Hold the applause

Call it my contribution to humanity

GAS BILLS

It's cold

The Hawk slipped in
the last three nights
and will not leave

Penetrated all defenses
first the windows
then the Doors
now even the Blankets

Squeezed the Sun
until light only
only light
when it comes

The House awakens
Boiler Roots
Pipe Branches
Radiator Leaves

November is its Spring

INVENTORY

4 matching forks
4 mismatched knives
7 cracked plates no
2 alike

3 pairs of low cuts
converse and black
5 worn out suits
hung on the rack

84 Honda white
tires old
70 Triumph
silver and gold

Victorian home
built in ought 2
"soffits need patching
porch needs work too"

"And (he continued
with no help from me)
it's just an investment
for years 1 thru 3"

"I'm out here looking
around O.S.U.
my kids are each candidates
for degrees 1 and 2"

Well the place is for sale
I said with a stutter
(I love this old house,
to hell with the gutter)

Way things have gone last
4 or 5 years
seems I must sell
regardless of tears

So in my own home
there they all stood
and tramped through my heart
him and his brood

Now if we count up
what each of us had
I suppose an observer
would multiply not add

And give him the nod
in category
he'd have the most
inventory

But what I saw
in the midst of my strife was
3 daughters huge and
1 very Fat wife.

ACCOUNTANT'S DILEMMA (PRO FORMA)

If you were told
the only thing to
pay
attention to was
what you were
paying
attention to
would you be distracted
from what you were
paying
attention to

If you were told
paying
attention to what you were
paying
attention to fully satisfied the
debts
owed to distraction
would you question the tellers credentials or
spend
your attention risking all
cost

For the projected
Balance sheet
Bottom line
of Peace

TRIBAL LIFE

The newspaper quoting
A famous movie director on
how he gets actors to engage in
STEAMY LOVE SCENES

It helps if they have a few drinks
before the shoot

Tobacco is sacred to Tribal people
Peyote is sacred to Tribal people
Marijuana is sacred to Tribal people
Alcohol they made it out of bugs to blood
is sacred to Tribal people

Sacredness

We put it everywhere
except in Sin

1993 JOKES

It was a morning like many others with
a coffee
a cigarette
a paper

The letter to the Editor said:
Keep the Sioux out of the Ohio Indian Council

Made me laugh.

Thought about
Tecumseh
Pontiac
Sitting Bull
Geronimo

Thought about them and
eachs counterpart who
standing on the West Bank of the Ohio
after 250 years of land succession
could not get together to
stop the flow

Seventy five years later maybe
a little more than one human lifetime
it was all gone

And this Indians about the
Western Sioux taking over
The Ohio Council of Indians

Kawabunga Kee Ma Sabe

INDIAN MOUNDS

We will count them Jim
as we go up
After twenty we stopped to rest
98° with a searing wind
Thirty more and another landing

Hand in Hand
Mother and son
sister and brother
girl and boy
woman and man
daughter and father
seventy-five and forty six

Earlier as I watched her walk
toward me from afar
grey and hesitant
I saw only the child
so fragile so innocent
so trusting so fearless

Stripped this time of
plenary power to
call up and call down
ferocious resource
against any force so foolish to
threaten any thing I called my own

Now only my arm to offer
Now only my time to spend

She does not mind

Found some shade
stopped again at eighty

leaning against the railings

Cant wait to see from the top
see the other side of this
but I have to rest here

In that time she would be borne
upon the shoulders of others
her feet never touching the ground

But we rest

Okay we can start again
and throwing off the years
she transcends the remaining steps
and the top we reach

Her hand
soft and small stays in mine and
we look

Below us stretches the
tree covered hills and valleys of Ohio

I am so sorry
M.O.M.
so so sorry

EPA

Premier re cycler
they all call me here
those homeless harmless gentle folk
collecting cans of beer

Hey it's not just cans
that get re cycled through
I also conscientiously create
long streams of yellow dew.

PASTURES

My foot went Bad
on me

and stayed Bad
for 3 weeks

Bad
like a Bad Boy
like a Bad Girl
like a Bad Dog

My vehicle wasn't
up to being up to it

Drove it like I heard
Cowboys
drove a cattle herd

making it
forcing it
pushing it
punishing it

for being Bad

DANDELIONS (AND CLOVER)

Ohio is the land of the omnipotent omniscient
mower
If it grows we will
mow
Bless those
unaddressed
unattended
overgrown
neglected
vacant fucking lots

DOGWOODS

This Spring I decided against vacation away
Last Spring I decided for vacation away

This Winter was long
Last Winter was harsh

This Spring I caught every flowerbloom and birdsong
Last Spring I missed them

The Dogwoods are out

In the late twilight and night their petals float
luminous white the ghostly separateness of the otherworld

This Spring I got drunk and talked to them
This Spring I got drunk and talked into the Earth

This Spring I said do not kill these people human
they are but children

This Spring give them one more chance
just one more chance

I know you are considering their end
I know you carry this power

Give them one more chance
just one more chance

This Spring they are only now awakening
give them one more chance

For I and my loved ones are them.

THE CARDINAL

Startled all my senses alerted
The Cardinal offered his song of Spring

outside my window
March to June
I awakened to his song of Spring

CHEER CHEER CHEER
CHEETER CHEETER CHEETER

But it was late September

and I knew he was singing his last song
until the Spring.

(LIFE IN) THE CITY

20 morning Dragonflies
(Like the 1st Cav.)
helicoptered the hill

15 afternoon Crows
cawed the Law

10 evening Swallows
swifted the sky
dolphining

Then
above my narrowed horizon
a forsure Falcon
8 miles high
held motionless

RIVETED BOLTED
my heart did take flight
my spirit did soar

just like you read about.

TWILIGHT

The in between.
       warmth & chill
       light & dark
the in between

awaiting the license
to follow the drink and
       Rest the face
       Shed the sound
       read the shadow
       ride the thought
       trace the tear
       hear the wound
       burst the laugh
       wonder the moon

wild night is calling.

APRIL (FOOL)

Aprilfool
you fool

April is April
cold it is and
cold it always
was

only a fool
says Aprilfool

fool you fool

April is
April

Fool.

RELATIONSHIPS

She said
>I'll just say it I love you
>I'm in love with you

She said
>I don't know whether I love you
>or I love being with you

She said
>I don't know what you feel
>what you feel about us I mean

She said
>I need the words to hear the words
>the lease on my heart is running out

He said
>you have been in relationship with men before
>three of them three years each

He said
>Have you not heard the words before
>Have you not said the words before

He said
>these words and most words have abandoned their
>value
>my words hold value

He said
>I told you I can not will not
>Love all the things you say you love

He said
>these words thrilled you
>although you said they hurt you

He said
>those words resonate your being
>that resonance is authentic trustworthy

He said
>they trilled in your soul

           like a mountain thrush in spring time
He said
           this is what I have to say
           this say is not bait for your sexual favor
He said
           listen your soul like you listen the word love
           and no word can abandon its value

No matter its source

ON THE LINE

With no capacity
for explanation
he tried to explain

chasing
hunting
tracking

the words

dancing in his head
just out of reach

tempting
taunting
tantalizing

he waited
still

Listening with the demanding silence
on the line

the words to

surrender
settle
satisfy

The demanding silence on the line

voicelessly.

TESTS

Didn't make the Grade

oh I aced the
Look test
Feel test
Smell test
Touch test
Laugh test
Cry test
even the Blood test

just passed the
Attention test
Call test
Ambition test
Credential test
Money test

but failed the Behavior test
(what about the curve) and

Didn't make the Grade.

DOROTHY WAS A HOOKER IN OZ

Out for a few jars with the Lads

In a bar
men and women
boys and girls
males and females

Eyeing with furtive glances
the Babes and vice versa
But we were 42 and 46

Naturally
the subject of getting Laid
arrived

He said
        10 months ago was his last time
        2 years had passed before that
        needed some time away from it
        But when opportunity knocked 10 months ago
        he cracked open that door

He said
        Found myself in bed fucking
        with a 40 yr old 4 kidded divorced woman
        Great body pretty smart dresser
        But jeezus clueless about the act

He said
        She made an unbelievable array of noises
        maybe it's me but doesn't she go to movies
        watch T.V. see ads
        they're all about sex and Fucking

He said

123

Hell they're all training films aren't they
Didn't she see them
If she did what did she see

Why is fucking such a goddamn mystery
Why don't they train us and them
Like driver's school algebra computers

Christ 35 years after Puberty
husband and 4 kids for 15
been divorced for 5

He said
        this is no one time thing
        happens more often than not
        I've been fucking for 25 years myself

Later
in my cups I thought
I can imagine what the female side of this is

Fundamentally
In my beer flavored mind it came this way
        Intrinsic Magic and Intrinsic Power
        Live in Sexual Intercourse Sexual interaction
        fucking as we say

        The very idea of openly creating a way
        a training of males and females
        in Sexual Intercourse Sexual Interaction would

        validate authenticate
        intrinsic magic and intrinsic power
        in the co operations of males and females

Magic and Power and Fucking
Witches and Spells and Sins

Lions and Tigers and Bears oh my

And then it came this way
   Sexual Intercourse sexual interaction Fucking
   are not designed as one being over an other being
   but as invitations avenues for exploration
   the discovery of the fearless self

   Sexual Intercourse Interaction Fucking is the
   transcendent unobstructed door opening upon
   the one remaining pathway to
   intrinsic magic and intrinsic power

   Fear is powerless to Block this Pathway

   He knew her in the Biblical way
   She knew him in the Biblical way
   They fucked spare me the they made love
   But they did approach knowing

And then it went this way
   The force of sexual intercourse interaction Fucking
   is the burst of light
   illuminating this fear darkened pathway

   to know an other
   be in an other
   be an other

   Organic bedrock power full
   as the ground is the soil is the growing
   The Essence of Creation the Magic

   But there is no training

   So at 13 we hit the Wall

That which has us says DO NOT
        Help them find the door
        Give them the keys
        Show them the light
        Guide them on this pathway

That which has us says
        Know one did this for you
        Look how you turned out

That which has us cowers
        quaking shuddering trembling
        at the face of
        our intrinsic power and magic

Now Look
        See how long and hard that which has us has
        worked to sustain and encourage the dishonoring of
        the one remaining pathway to knowing one an other

Yes look
        See how you turned out me us them and
        Dorothy
        the lion
        the scarecrow
        the tin man
        the wizard

Magic and Power and Fucking
Witches and Spells and Sins
Lions and Tigers and Bears

Oh my.

IT TAKES ONE TO KNOW ONE

Saw a talk show
women forty and over
each of them
attractive but
out of men
asked to itemize each's perfect man
sensitive
caring
gentle
strong
fun
understanding
do things
Christ heard that song since I was 15
thirty one years

It takes one to know one

To each my thought so find another woman
but females know women
do not carry these in any greater degree than men
perhaps less

the evolved measure of self value
the amount of concession one gifts
to anothers inconsiderateness

This is sensitivity
this is gentleness
this is caring
this is strength
this is fun
this is listening
this is understanding

127

This is bullshit

Self value does not reside in withheld
pussy
and then gracing the concessionaire with
access

You want a man go to a
BAR
There you will find fifty to one hundred males
in all flavors

If you do not want to be othertouched
go to where the secret predators feed
The supermarket the library the group
the seminar the work the personals
the too old the too young the marrieds
the church the social the status
the the the the the the

go to
THE BAR
quit feeding
THE MANIPULATION

TEACH AND LEARN

Warriors and Heroes are there
This lifetime they'll let you in

It takes one to know one.

FOOTBALL

Ohio State Football
don't we love it all
the pagentry the color
that comes around each fall.

There is this old song
adopted by the crowd
all sing and swing and move to
makes us feel so proud.

I know you know the tune
that's held enduring fame
but now's the time for courage
and stake a warrior's claim.

To see the actual words
the meaning each contains
as they dance within the music
like drops within the rain:

Sloopy lives in a very bad part of town
and everybody yeah tries to put my Sloopy down

Sloopy I don't care what your daddy do
cause you know Sloopy girl
I'm in love with you

Sloopy let your hair down girl
let it hang down on me

Sloopy let your hair down
let it hang down on me

Come on Sloopy
come on come on

well come on Sloopy
come on come on

Well it feels so good
come on come on

yeah it feels so good
come on come on

Shake it shake it shake it
Sloopy

Come on come
Shake it shake it shake it yeah

Hang on Sloopy
Sloopy hang on

Waits and Measures

Don't know why
I've been thinkin about
Jesus
Seems so many of us humans
have put such a burden on him

How come nobody every thinks about him
sittin on the can
readin a scroll
lookin for a little peace and quiet

Now he wasn't a stranger to money either
was he
He needed a few sheckles now and then
for a glass of wine or a good square

Best I can figure he wasn't a
Borrower
Didn't have a job unless he moonlighted as a
Carpenter

Don't remember exactly but one miracle apiece
for wine and food
How'd he get them for the other 363 days

And another thing
how can a guy with no wife or girlfriend or kids
33 years old
get so caught up in our family values

Don't think he was a homo
but you know circumstantial evidence
hung around exclusively with men
that's the way I heard it

But then he did have a few
Hookers
The way I see it hookers don't have to hook
unless they're not getting a
fair shot
at the available sheckles without getting
married to get them

Ole Jesus must have
Shared some of the loot with them
sos they didn't have to choose
between getting married and hooking

Don't suppose there were many other
good jobs available back then
But I don't know maybe
cooking and cleaning
secretarying and waitressing
were bigger payers than they are now

You know some one comes up with
a few good ideas about getting along
in this here world
and the next thing you know people want to
hear them
hear them
hear them

And then they start
following this someone around and
make him hold them as if he owned them and
was responsible for making them work

This wouldn't be so bad if it was
just one lifetime
but man for 2000 years
now that's a burden

Why it would make this some one sorry
he even thought them up and
that they were so good that he put on a show
to get folks attention and

If this some one died and
then had a chance to come back to
this here earth
I'd bet he'd be thinkin long and hard
about takin it
Anyway this Jesus thing came up
don't know why

It's noon
time for lunch

HIDING

My talk offends you

Pussy and cocks
drugs and trips
Booze and cigarettes

Here is what offends you

Hate and Anger
jealousy and judgment
prejudice and fear

Belief and Truth

Run to the closet
under the bed
anywhere each will
NEVER
NEVER
EVER
Find you

But do not hide

It won't be easy

SPECIAL

You are special
Your children are special

Your children are special
You are special

Special

You are
children
you are

Special

You deserve a rest

take a nap

<u>HERE THERE AND EVERY WHERE</u>

Am I
here
or some
where
else

If I am somewhere else
where
am
I

or am I
Here

sleep

used to be full of
dreams

now just full of
sleep.

YIKES

You wait all your life
to kill some thing
and it turns out to be
something you love.

LABELS
(CALVIN KLEIN)

The label I carry
is not of sword & shield

The label I carry is of
grey gray

Would if I could choose black or white
white or black

I would choose black or white
white or black

draw the sword raise the shield
strike the blow

against black or white
white or black

The label I carry
kills not another

slowly painfully it kills
not the me you see
but the me that sees.

<u>DIS-TRACTIONS</u>

no do to work
no go to place
no take to side
no win to race

no eat to food
no drink to beer
no light to dark
no face to fear

no waste to time
no right to wrong
no say to word
no sing to song

no be to way
no hide to run
no on to off
no up to down

no know to no
no know to yes
no dust to dust
no life to death

no lose to hope
no below to above

no love to hate
and
no hate to love

EVEN A BLIND HOG

ACORN BEER ON TAP

ROOTS UP AN ACORN

By James Moore Herald

SECRETS IN THE MALE UNIVERSE

www.ingramcontent.com/pod-product-compliance
Lightning Source LLC
Chambersburg PA
CBHW071301130626
46556CB00003B/1413